Great Women in History

Pocahontas

by Erin Edison

Consulting Editor: Gail Saunders-Smith, PhD

Consultant: Dr. Brie Swenson Arnold
Assistant Professor of History
Coe College, Cedar Rapids, Iowa

CAPSTONE PRESS
a capstone imprint

Pebble Books are published by Capstone Press,
1710 Roe Crest Drive, North Mankato, Minnesota 56003.
www.capstonepub.com

Library of Congress Cataloging-in-Publication Data
Edison, Erin.
  Pocahontas / by Erin Edison.
      p. cm.—(Pebble books. great women in history)
  Includes bibliographical references and index.
  ISBN 978-1-62065-074-5 (library binding)
  ISBN 978-1-62065-861-1 (paperback)
  ISBN 978-1-4765-1629-5 (eBook PDF)
1. Pocahontas, d. 1617—Juvenile literature. 2. Powhatan women—Biography—
Juvenile literature. 3. Smith, John, 1580-1631—Juvenile literature. I. Title.
  E99.P85.P571433E45 2013
  975.5′01092—dc23
  [B]   2012033473

Note to Parents and Teachers

The Great Women in History set supports national social studies
standards related to people and culture. This book describes
and illustrates Pocahontas. The images support early readers in
understanding the text. The repetition of words and phrases helps
early readers learn new words. This book also introduces early
readers to subject-specific vocabulary words, which are defined
in the Glossary section. Early readers may need assistance to read
some words and to use the Table of Contents, Glossary, Read More,
Internet Sites, and Index sections of the book.

Printed in the United States of America in North Mankato, Minnesota.
012014   007957R

Table of Contents

around 1595

born

Early Life

Pocahontas is a symbol of the early meeting of American Indian and English peoples. She was born around 1595. Her father, Chief Powhatan, led 30 tribes known as the Powhatan Confederacy. They lived in what is now Virginia.

 around 1595

born

 1607

the English build
Jamestown

Growing up, Pocahontas learned to grow food and make pottery. She built houses and cared for other children. Life changed for Pocahontas and all Powhatan peoples in 1607. English colonists arrived and built Jamestown.

around 1595

born

1607

the English build
Jamestown

Young Adult

The English and Powhatan traded with each other. The English needed food, and the Powhatan wanted copper and tools. Pocahontas sometimes went to Jamestown. During these visits, she met Captain John Smith, a leader of the colonists.

◀ Captain John Smith

 around 1595

born

 1607

the English build
Jamestown

Although they traded with each other, the English and Powhatan didn't always get along. More colonists began moving onto American Indian land. Fighting broke out between the two groups.

around 1595

born

1607

the English build
Jamestown

1613

kidnapped by
the English

In 1613, after more fighting, the English kidnapped Pocahontas. They told Chief Powhatan to give them corn and other goods in return for Pocahontas. But in order to protect his people, Chief Powhatan could not give in to the English.

a drawing of Chief Powhatan by Captain John Smith

around 1595

born

1607

the English build
Jamestown

1613

kidnapped by
the English

14

Adulthood

Pocahontas remained with the English. They expected her to read and speak English. She was told to dress like an Englishwoman.

 around 1595

born

 1607

the English build
Jamestown

 1613

kidnapped by
the English

During her time with the English, Pocahontas married Englishman John Rolfe. Both the Powhatan and the English hoped this marriage would bring peace. For a few years, there was peace between the two groups.

◀ colonists and the Powhatan trading

1614

marries John Rolfe

around 1595

born

1607

the English build
Jamestown

1613

kidnapped by
the English

In 1616 Pocahontas, John Rolfe, and their son traveled to London, England. Pocahontas met the king and queen and saw John Smith again. She hoped her meetings with the English would help them respect her people.

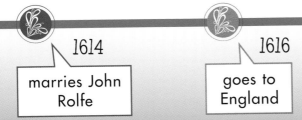

1614
marries John Rolfe

1616
goes to England

around 1595

born

1607

the English build
Jamestown

1613

kidnapped by
the English

20

Remembering Pocahontas

Pocahontas became sick while in England. She died there in March 1617. Today Pocahontas is remembered for an important role. She understood both English and American Indian ways of life.

1614
marries John Rolfe

1616
goes to England

1617
dies

Glossary

American Indian—a person related to the first people who lived in North or South America

chief—the leader of a group of people

colonist—a person who lives in a colony; a colony is land ruled by another country

respect—to admire and have a good opinion of someone; respect means to treat others the way you would like to be treated

symbol—something that reminds people of something else

trade—to exchange one item for another; American Indians traded corn and fish to the English settlers in exchange for beads, tools, and copper

tribe—a group of people who share the same family members, way of life, and laws

Read More

Adams, Colleen. *The True Story of Pocahontas.* What Really Happened? New York: PowerKids Press, 2009.

Harkins, Susan Sales, and William H. Harkins. *Pocahontas.* What's So Great about...? Mitchell Lane Publishers, 2009.

Smith, Andrea P. *Pocahontas and John Smith.* New York: PowerKids Press, 2012.

Internet Sites

FactHound offers a safe, fun way to find Internet sites related to this book. All of the sites on FactHound have been researched by our staff.

Here's all you do:

Visit *www.facthound.com*

Type in this code: 9781620650745

Check out projects, games and lots more at
www.capstonekids.com

23

Index

Word Count: 299
Grade: 1
Early-Intervention Level: 25

Editorial Credits
Erika Shores, editor; Alison Thiele, designer; Wanda Winch, media researcher;
Jennifer Walker, production specialist

Photo Credits
Alamy: North Wind Picture Archives, 8, 12; Corbis: Bettmann, 4; Library of
Congress: Prints and Photographs Division, cover, 1, 14, 18; National Parks
Service/Colonial National Historical Park/Sidney E. King, artist, 6, 10, 16;
Shutterstock: Fears, cover design, spirit of America, 20